# American Soldier
# Proud and Free

# by Kimberly Jo Simac
# Illustrations by Donna Goeddaeus

This book is dedicated to
God my Father.
Who has always been with me,
giving me so many wonderful gifts.
The greatest gift of all is being born an American.

A special thank you to:
Kitty Sookochoff
Matt Van Skyhawk
Dara Maillette
Abbey Maillette

Published by
**Great Northern Adventure Co., Inc.**
**3860 Kula Vista Drive - P.O. Box 961**
**Eagle River, WI 54521**
**715-479-8784**
**bk951@verizon.net**
**www.gnaco.com**

Layout and Editing by:
Great Northern Adventure Co., Inc.
Abbey Maillette
Dara Maillette

Photography by:
Lakeside Studios
Kitty Sookochoff
715-479-2974
www.lakesidephoto.com

Printing Managed by
RR Donnelley
Menasha, WI 54952-0060

Library of Congress Cataloging-in-Publication Data
Simac, Kimberly Jo

ISBN-978-0-9763931-2-2

ISBN-0-9763931-2-3

Printed in China
1st Printing

To all who

love America...

My favorite picture
hanging on the wall.....

.....is the one of
my Grandpa
standing
proud and tall.

Dad always tells stories
of how he served
for you and me.

So that all
of us here could
have freedom guaranteed.

When I go to school
the first thing I see,
is the American flag
flying over me.

We say the
"Pledge of Allegiance."
I hold my hand
over my heart.

The words
"liberty and justice for all"
are one of the best parts.

I love history.
It is my favorite class.
There are
so many great stories
of heroes from the past.

How soldiers gave their lives
to set others free.

How brave men changed
the world so God's
plan could be.

I have a tree fort
in my backyard.

I like to play Army
and practice
standing guard.

I practice marching forward,
I practice standing tall.

I have to stand guard and be ready,
should my enemies pay me a call.

At night
I say my prayers.
I ask
God
to find a way.....

To keep the world a happy place

where all children can be safe to play.

Dad
says there
may come a time
when we may
have to say.....

....."This land belongs to
you and me,
and it might take a war
to keep it that way!"

I would be proud
to be a soldier.
I would want
to do what's right.

I would want
to protect my family,
even if it means a fight.

I want to
be like my
Grandpa
and his buddies
from the war.....

Because I believe
America
is something worth
fighting for.

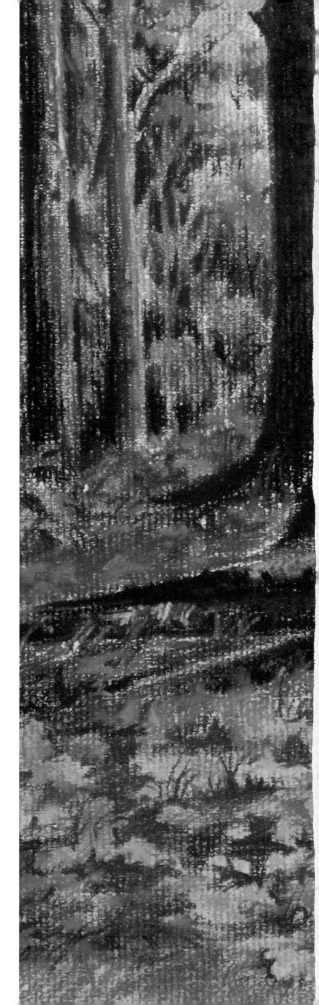